For Charlotte, with all
my love xx - TC

For Matt, Lou and Marcie - JC

LITTLE TIGER PRESS
1 The Coda Centre, 189 Munster Road,
London SW6 6AW
www.littletiger.co.uk

First published in Great Britain 2014

Text copyright © Tracey Corderoy 2014
Illustrations copyright © Jane Chapman 2014

Visit Jane Chapman at www.ChapmanandWarnes.com

ISBN 978-1-84895-904-0
LTP/1400/0893/0314

10 9 8 7 6 5 4 3 2 1

THE MAGICAL
SNOW
GARDEN

Tracey Corderoy

Jane Chapman

LITTLE TIGER PRESS
London

Far away, where
snowflakes twinkled, lived
a little penguin called Wellington.

Wellington loved his snowy world - sliding
down hills, digging for treasure, and sharing
books with his very best friend.

"Rosemary, look at this **garden**," he cried.
"It's amazing! Let's grow one just like it!"

"PERCY!" called Wellington. "I'm going to grow a **garden**!"

"Oh, Wellington," chuckled Percy, "that's **impossible**!"

"We don't **grow** things, we **fish**," Mabel smiled.

"I wanted to fly once," Ivor explained. "But penguins **can't** fly. And flowers **can't** grow in the snow - it's just **too** cold!"

"But **Ivor**," said Wellington, "how will we know unless we **try?**"

Wellington's books all said the same.
To grow flowers he needed **seeds**.
But there weren't any seeds in their snowy, white world. Not one.
"There **MUST** be a way," Rosemary chirped as they shared a biscuit.

Wellington looked at the shiny, blue wrapper.

With a fold here and there, it was just like . . .

"A bluebell!" cried Wellington. "I can **make** a garden instead!"

So Wellington filled his biggest net with things to make his garden: wrappers and buttons, Ivor's old clock bits, and pearly-white seashells from Rosemary's faraway travels.

For **days** Wellington whizzed about — folding and twirling . . .

glittering and gluing . . .

digging and planting, **until** . . .

"Ta daaa!"

Now all of the wrappers were beautiful flowers, all the buttons bright bumblebees. Clockwork trees dotted the hills, sprinkled in snow-white blossom.

"Look!" Percy pointed.
"Gosh!" Mabel gasped.
"HE'S DONE IT!"
Ivor smiled.

"Wellington's made a **magical snow** garden!" they cried.

But the garden had no wall to
keep out the wind. And that
very night a storm blew in.
It whipped and whirled
and roared. WHOOSH!

And Wellington's garden was blown away . . .

. . . every last petal.

"Never mind," said Mabel.
"You tried your best."
They brought him warm milk
and biscuits. But Wellington
shook his head. "No thanks,"
he sighed.

Just then, he heard a flutter of wings and Rosemary dropped something in his lap.

Slowly, Wellington smoothed out the shiny, blue wrapper. Then he folded it, just so.

"The first bluebell for my next garden!" Wellington nodded.

This time Wellington's friends helped to make his lovely new garden.

Percy built a wall to keep out the wind, Mabel made a beautiful fountain and Ivor's trees had cuckoos that sang!

Then Rosemary flew off to tell the world of her friend's **amazing garden** . . .

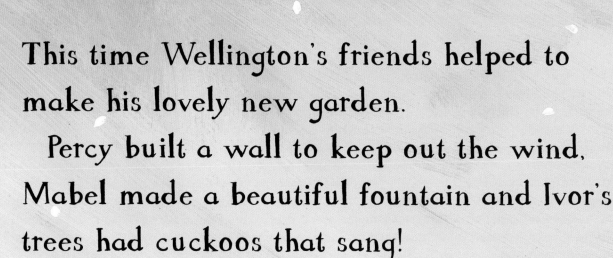

. . . and the **whole wide world** came hurrying to see it!

There were bright pink flamingos, koalas and camels, and elephants with trumpeting trunks.

There were zebras, giraffes and bouncing kangaroos!

"**Wow!**" Wellington gasped.

"Wellington!" called Ivor. "You were right! You never know what you can do until you try!"

"Hooray for Wellington," everyone cheered, "and his magical garden in the snow!"